BIKER MICE™ FROM MARS

CHILL ZONE

BIKER MICE FROM **MARS**™

CHILL ZONE

CLARE DANNATT

MAMMOTH

First published in 1994 by Mammoth
an imprint of Reed Children's Books
Michelin House, 81 Fulham Road, London SW3 6RB
and Auckland, Melbourne, Singapore and Toronto

ISBN 0 7497 1701 7

A CIP catalogue record for this title is available from the British Library

Printed and bound in Great Britain
by Cox & Wyman Ltd, Reading, Berks

Chapter One

The wintry Chicago sky was dark with snow. A bitter wind nipped the faces of the Christmas shoppers hurrying along the streets that were brightly lit with decorations. On a street corner a little group of carol singers stamped their feet as they sang 'Deck the halls with boughs of holly!' They sang so sweetly that even the coldest passers-by paused for a moment to listen.

High above the singers, someone else was listening and watching from a darkened office window. 'Carol singers,' he murmured. 'How quaint. Perhaps they would care for a hot drink to warm them in this winter weather.' The shadowy figure picked up a large coffee pot from a table – and emptied it out of the window.

'Hey! Who did that?' yelled the carol singers, breaking off from their chorus as warm coffee cascaded over their heads. Above them a window shut noiselessly.

Inside the office the unknown Scrooge chuckled softly to himself. 'Yes indeed, this is the season for sharing . . . And now I must get to work on my present for Plutark.' For this was no crazy Chicago character, but Lawrence Limburger, evil warlord from Plutark. His one aim was to restore the fortunes of that distant planet – and he would stop at nothing to achieve it.

Limburger pressed a button on a video monitor. 'Karbunkle!' he ordered, as his scientific adviser appeared on the screen.

'Seasonal greetings, your Big Cheesiness,' came the reply.

'Plutark needs ice, Karbunkle,' said Limburger briskly. 'Lots of it. And now! Are those Snosuckers ready yet?'

'Awaiting your command, your Ice Creaminess,' replied Karbunkle smoothly.

'Excellent! Now we can proceed with my plan to pilfer this planet's precious precipitation.'

'You mean steal the snow?' asked Karbunkle.

'Exactly!' Limburger chortled. 'By the time we have completed operations, Chicago will have had the blackest, bleakest Christmas within living memory!'

Chapter Two

On the outskirts of the city, the snow lay deep and crisp and even. In a large field a bunch of small children were playing excitedly with three strange-looking characters. The Biker Mice From Mars, Chicago's zaniest troubleshooters, were taking time out from crime-solving to have fun with the kids from the local orphanage. Throttle, Modo and Vinnie were making more noise than all the kids put together. Charley, their constant companion and motorcycle mechanic, looked on in amusement.

'You Biker guys pretend to be macho and tough,' she laughed, 'but underneath you're soft as snow!'

'Nah – we're macho and tough,' said Vinnie. 'Aaargh!' Vinnie tumbled over backwards as a small child shot past him on a sled, sending his biker helmet flying. Vinnie lobbed a playful snowball after the child, and soon the air was thick with happy shrieks and flying snowballs.

In another part of the snowfield, hidden from view by a hill, some more serious business was going on. Limburger and Karbunkle stood watching an army of strange machines at work. Like outsized vacuum cleaners, they chugged over the field, sucking up snow into their interiors, then ejecting perfectly compressed cubes of snow. The snow bales tumbled into a huge Plutarkian Transporter Tunnel which glowed eerily.

'Congratulations, my dear Karbunkle,' beamed Limburger. 'The Snosuckers are working perfectly. Even as we speak, the Earth's frozen fluid is gathering in space, being stored ready for shipment to my dear Plutark.'

Limburger was right. In the far reaches of outer space, a Plutarkian menial was standing on guard by the other end of the Transporter Tunnel, out of which the huge ice cubes from Chicago fell into an enormous storage bin.

Back on Earth, Limburger was ecstatic. 'Augment the acceleration, dear Doctor,' he gurgled.

Karbunkle looked blank. 'Um – what do you mean, exactly, your High Rankness?'

'Simple, you scientific simpleton!' Limburger barked, suddenly purple with fury. 'MAKE THEM GO FASTER!' He grabbed a hand-held control from Karbunkle and jabbed impatiently at a button. The Snosuckers clanked faster and faster, gobbling up snow at breakneck speed.

Back on the other side of the hill, the Biker Mice were still throwing snowballs without a care in the world. Suddenly, above their squeals of merriment, they heard a strange clanking noise. Glancing around in the direction of the noise, they saw hordes of the strange snow harvesters advancing over the brow of the hill, knocking down and devouring trees, snow and everything in their path. The Biker Mice and children gawped.

'What kinda snowman would drive those snowmobiles?' breathed Modo.

'I don't know,' said Throttle. 'But they look like mouse-munchers if anything does.'

The mindless machines roared towards the little group, jaws gaping. They were surrounded!

The Biker Mice lost no time. They leapt onto their bikes. 'Get them kids to safety, Charley!' commanded Modo, revving like fury.

But it was no use. The bikes were immediately bogged down in the soft snow. Vinnie fired his jets: his bike leapt up out of the snow and onto one of the kids' abandoned sleds. 'Hey bro's, I've joined the jet sled!' Vinnie shouted. The toboggan set off wildly. 'Rock and slide!' shrieked Vinnie.

Throttle switched his bike to all-terrain mode. Whump! The tyres inflated like giant balloons and he shot after Vinnie – who was having a few problems steering his sled. A Snosucker chugged towards him. 'Whoa!' panted Vinnie, dodging out of the machine's path at the last minute.

Now it was Modo's turn. He fired his bike-laser and roared off through the snowbank as the laser melted a path for his cycle. Vinnie and Throttle soon followed his lead, and the three friends blazed a trail right into a snowbank. Whoom! The bro's came blasting out the other side, straight into the path of the advancing Snosuckers.

Vinnie tried his vape cannon, but the recoil sent him spinning sideways. Throttle crouched low on his bike, roared up a hill, made a tremendous jump and bounced off a Snosucker. The impact sent the Sucker blundering off course. It crashed into a group of other Suckers. Wham! Crash! They exploded, sending the Biker Mice and bits of machinery flying through the air.

'Dig this, bro's – it's deep!' hollered Throttle, landing on a snowbank with such force that he disappeared inside it.

Modo shot right through another bank, and out the other side on to a frozen pond. Wheee! He skittered over the pond, then CRACK! Modo and his motorbike plunged through the surface of the ice, leaving him waist-high in the icy water.

Throttle struggled free from his pile of

snow. 'I don't know where those machines come from,' he declared, 'but it's time to chill 'em out.'

Foosh! Zap! Zappow! Throttle let his laser gun rip, blasting and blowing the Snosuckers to bits.

Limburger and Karbunkle stood in the field, now stripped back to bare earth by the Snosuckers. Karbunkle frowned as his remote control beeped wildly. 'Something is destroying the Snosuckers,' he muttered.

'These days "something" always seems to be those bothersome Biker Mice,' said Limburger between gritted teeth. 'Recall the Snosuckers immediately!'

Karbunkle jabbed his forefinger at the buttons on his control.

Down in the lower field, the three friends watched as the Snosuckers – what was left of them – suddenly reversed gears and ground back the way they had come.

'They're turnin' tail,' said Vinnie with satisfaction.

'Shame – I coulda used some exercise to warm me up,' shivered Modo, shaking icicles off his tail.

Throttle raised his eyebrows. 'Don't worry, comrade. If those machines come from Limburger, things'll get pretty hot pretty soon.'

Chapter Three

Deep inside his laboratory, Karbunkle was tinkering with a Snosucker. Limburger paced up and down. 'The Suckers must be armed with full weaponry, my good Doctor. I want to teach those Biker Mice a lesson they'll never forget. They must learn how foolish it is to meddle with the property of Lawrence Limburger, Esquire.'

Karbunkle sniggered. 'Fear not, your High Cheesiness – they will. And furthermore, I have something to show you which you may find intriguing.'

A video screen lit up to reveal the unmistakeable shapes of Charley and the Biker Mice, herding a group of small children to the safety of their orphanage.

'Interesting activity recorded by the Snosucker monitoring system, your Cheesiness,' said Karbunkle. 'Notice the Mice's fondness for little children.'

Limburger rubbed his hands together. 'Yes, it seems our rodent friends have a sentimental soft spot. And a soft spot is a weakness which I might be able to exploit...' He broke off abruptly.

'What's that?' he snapped, pointing out of the window.

Karbunkle frowned. 'That's the sun, your Mellow Richness.'

Limburger seethed. 'I know it's the sun, you sycophant. What's it doing there?'

'Shining?' gulped Karbunkle.

Limburger ground his teeth and rolled his eyes. 'It's melting the snow,' he exploded. 'Melted snow is useless to me. Plutark needs ICE.'

Karbunkle mopped his brow. 'Worry not, your Esteemed Excellence. I have just the villain to assist us. Observe!'

Karbunkle zapped the remote control of a Transporter machine with trembling fingers. There was a blinding flash of light and crackle of static – a short stocky woman had materialised in the laboratory. She waddled forward towards Karbunkle.

'Greetinks Doktor Karbunkle,' she warbled in a heavy German accent. 'I alvays said ve vould meet again!'

Limburger was not impressed. 'Who is this diminutive dimwit?' he snapped.

'This is the Weathermeister,' said Karbunkle proudly. 'She'll have Chicago icebound in no time.'

'She couldn't even ice a cake!' scoffed Limburger.

The Weathermeister glared at him and waved her hands contemptuously. A weather map of the very laboratory they were standing in appeared between her fingers. The Weathermeister slapped a cloud symbol over the part of the map showing Limburger. 'Today's forecast shows heffy rainstorms over Limburger Central,' she explained.

No sooner had she spoken the words than a small black cloud appeared over

Limburger's head and began raining heavily on him.

'What's going on?' gasped Limburger.

BOOM! came the reply from a small lightning bolt which struck him to the ground.

The master criminal struggled to his feet. 'Weathermeister,' he spluttered. 'You're hired.'

Chapter Four

The Weathermeister, Karbunkle and Limburger stood on the roof of Limburger Tower. The sun shone down on them – but all around the tower a blizzard raged and the wind howled – Chicago had become a chill zone.

The Weathermeister was studying a map of the city.

'Lots of ice!' Limburger reminded her.

'Uff course,' she replied. 'Record lows, heffy snows and frrreeeezing blizzards for

Chicago the Vindy City, eh? Except for right here on Limburger Tower, vere it's a nice sunny day, ja?'

'Wonderful work, wonderful,' exclaimed Limburger, now completely converted to the Weathermeister's charms. 'It almost makes me want to give up crime,' he added, 'and go into the tourist trade!' The others gasped. 'Almost...' he continued thoughtfully, 'but not quite.'

Limburger stopped daydreaming and turned to the matter in hand. 'I wonder how those puny little orphan brats are getting on?' he asked gleefully.

'Not too well I would wager, your Wickedness,' smiled Karbunkle.

'I hope not,' laughed Limburger. 'Because they are my nice juicy bait for those foolish Biker Mice.'

Vinnie glanced out of the window of the Last Chance Garage. All he could see was a mass of whirling snow. He whistled and shook his head. 'Dreamin' of a white Christmas is one thing – this is more like a nightmare.'

'You're not kidding,' agreed Charley, glancing at the TV news while they all fixed their bikes. She tightened the last few nuts that would convert a bike to snow-mobile mode, and stared at the TV screen. 'That's the orphanage those sweet kids live in,' she said.

The friends fell silent to hear the news.

'With no food, heat or running water and the snow blocking all relief efforts, things are looking very bad indeed for the children of this orphanage,' said the TV announcer grimly. The orphanage was faintly visible behind her in the driving snow. 'All any of us can do now is pray for a miracle,' she ended.

The Biker Mice looked at one another determinedly.

'That means us,' said Modo.

'Miracles Incorporated,' added Vinnie.

'Neither hail nor snow nor Plutarkian plots will stop these Biker Mice from saving those kids,' declared Throttle. 'Let's rock!'

'And RIDE!' shouted the others, leaping onto their bikes. And with rear wheels flaring, they blasted out into the snow.

The Biker Mice plunged through the streets which lay neck-deep in snow, their spiked treads ripping up the road and their skis throwing out great rooster tails of spray.

'Dashing through the snow,' sang Throttle lustily.

'On a 300 horse-power sleigh,' piped up Modo.

'O'er the streets we go,' Vinnie joined in.

'Whip tail all the way!' chorused the three of them.

They roared past a man struggling to dig his car out of a snowdrift. The bikes blasted the snow clean away, leaving the astonished motorist gaping after them. Throttle gave him the Biker salute. 'Ride free, Citizen!' he called.

Someone else was watching the progress of the motorcycles with interest. From the heights of his tower, Limburger was peering through his high-powered binoculars. 'Those rampaging rodents have revealed themselves at last,' he declared with satisfaction. 'Ready to mash some mice?' he asked the Weathermeister.

'Uff course!' she replied with relish, pulling her map out of the air and stabbing her finger at the orphanage site. 'Huge hailstones comink up right here!'

* * *

The bikes roared on towards the orphanage at high speed, clearing the road around them. Behind them lumbered a convoy of relief trucks.

'Merry Christmas to all!' bawled the furry freedom fighters as they went. 'And a happy...'

CRASH! A giant hailstone smashed down beside Modo, who swerved just in time. 'Watch out!' he warned. 'That was no Christmas bauble.' Soon they were all dodging and weaving about the road as hailstones the size of bowling balls bounced down around them. Up ahead, all of them could see the stones smashing down on the orphanage.

'Them kids are in trouble,' shouted Modo.

'You said it, bro',' agreed Throttle.

'We gotta do something,' cried Vinnie.

They ploughed on towards the orphanage as best as they could. Inside the building they could hear children screaming and crying as the stones battered down on their besieged home. 'This weather ain't natural,' gasped Modo.

'Must be some sorta trap,' Vinnie agreed.

'In that case,' said Throttle decisively, 'let's make it a trapshoot, bro's. Follow me.' Throttle blasted forward on his bike, firing up into the sky with his laser pistol.

BLAM! BLAM! The Biker Mice blew the hailstones out of the air as they rode up to the orphanage.

'Santa may come down the chimney,' Throttle observed.

'But we prefer the front door!' whooped Modo, breaking his way in.

Inside, a group of pathetic children and their carer huddled around a Christmas tree. BOOM! A hailstone came flying through the roof, smashing the tree to smithereens. The orphans started to cry – then they saw the Biker Mice and began to laugh instead.

'It's the Biker Guys,' grinned one little girl.

'Yeah!' they all cheered.

There was no time to waste. Scooping up the children and their carer onto their bikes, the supercharged threesome shot out of the orphanage to safety.

Chapter Five

From the shelter of a rocky overhang the children and their rescuers watched the last few hailstones fizzle out into nothing.

'Looks like the storm's over,' said Vinnie at last.

'For now,' continued Throttle darkly.

'You O.K.?' Modo asked the children.

'Yes...but...' said a boy, looking sad and pointing into the distance. 'Our home is all smashed up.'

'And it's almost Christmas,' added an older girl.

The hailstone heroes sniffed and blew their noses. 'It's just like that old movie,' gulped Modo.

'We'll fix it. Somehow,' Throttle promised the kids. He took Vinnie and Modo aside. 'I gotta feeling that storm was no accident,' he muttered.

'I'd say you're right,' said Vinnie, pointing urgently into the distance. 'Look!'

Throttle and Modo squinted. Nothing was visible through the swirls of murky snow. Then they saw what Vinnie had seen. Limburger Tower shone like a beacon in the darkness, lit up in a shaft of brilliant sunshine.

'The Big Cheese is makin' sure his toes stay toasty,' said Vinnie grimly.

'He must've found a way to control the weather,' said Modo, just a little impressed.

'I knew this whole set-up was a trap,' Throttle said.

The bro's were silent for a moment – then flicked their tails and twirled their whiskers. Action!

'Come on,' urged Vinnie. 'It's time to turn that Cheddar Gorge into Baked Alaska!'

'Let's rock,' screeched Throttle, revving his engine.

'And RIDE!' they all chorused together.

And with a deafening blast of heavy metal, the Biker Mice were on their way.

Limburger put another dab of suntan cream on his nose and took a swig of iced tea. 'Let's see how the rest of the Windy City is faring,' he chuckled, peering through his binoculars at the snowstorm raging a few metres away.

But Limburger was in for a nasty shock. 'BLAST!' he yelled, knocking over his tea. 'Those bothersome Biker Mice have beaten the bombardment.' Through his field glasses Limburger watched the unmistakeable shapes of the Biker Mice tearing towards Limburger Tower, kicking up huge fantails of snow with their bikes.

Karbunkle grabbed the binoculars. 'Yes, you are right – as usual, your fragrant fulsomeness. And they seem to know you are involved in Chicago's greatest ever weather disaster,' he added nervously.

Limburger wiped his brow. 'It's hot up here,' he gulped. 'Perhaps it might be wise to have departed before they arrive.

'How is Lake Michigan at the moment, Weathermeister?'

'Almost a solid block uff ice, Cheese-meister,' replied the weather-witch with satisfaction.

Limburger ducked suddenly as a Biker missile flew towards him. 'Excellent,' he said from his crouched position. 'Shall we depart?' Another missile exploded by his left foot. 'Without further ado?'

The Weathermeister snapped her fingers by way of reply and Zing! an extraordinary craft with a weather vane stuck on top of it appeared on the roof. 'Step aboard my Veatherplane,' invited the Weathermeister.

Limburger and Karbunkle lost no time. Soon the weather vane was whirling, and the craft lifted away from the top of the tower.

Chapter Six

The Biker Mice rumbled along at high speed, firing missiles as they rode.

'You've gone too far this time, Cheese-burger,' ranted Modo.

'Yeah,' added Vinnie. 'No one messes with little kids when the Biker Mice From Mars are around.'

Throttle skidded to a halt. 'Whoa! Hold your fire, bro's.' The others screeched to a halt alongside Throttle. Above them they saw the Weatherplane, gliding away from Limburger Tower with its cargo of villains.

'Our birdie has flown,' groaned Throttle.

'So?' said Vinnie. 'He's gotta come down somewhere.'

Modo flipped out his arm cannon. 'It may not be Christmas yet,' he said grimly, 'but I'm sure gonna make my presence felt.'

Throttle grinned. 'I hear you, bro'. Let's dash away, dash away, dash away all!'

Frooom! The bikes blasted resolutely after the departing Weatherplane.

Limburger, Karbunkle and the Weathermeister hovered over Lake Michigan. Limburger grinned at the vast expanse of ice beneath him.

'Excellent. This ice should complete my first shipment to Plutark with ease,' he gloated. 'Karbunkle!'

'Yes, your Over-ripeness?'

'Send in the Snosuckers.'

'Of course. At once.'

With a crackle of static from his transporter module, Karbunkle summoned the army of Snosuckers. The grim machines materialised on the lake and began to bite great chunks out of the ice. Water bubbled up from underneath, but froze immediately in the piercing cold.

Limburger was ecstatic. 'Excellent, excellent. Now I can freeze all the water on Earth and steal every last icicle for Plutark. And when all the water is in my control, the Earth's leaders will beg me to take their precious natural resources, in exchange for one drop of water!' He chuckled wickedly, his breath condensing into huge, billowing clouds. 'It's cruel,' he continued happily. 'It's clever – it's – aargh!'

The Biker Mice had arrived. They burst through a snowdrift with all weapons firing.

'This party doesn't look like much fun,' yelled Vinnie.

'So we've come along to break the ice,' shrieked Modo.

Boom! Boom! The villains inside the Weatherplane ducked the volley of frost-busting missiles.

'Why must those Mice always mess up my manouevres?' snarled Limburger.

Karbunkle gripped his control tightly. 'Don't worry your Red Leicestership – watch this!'

Suddenly the Snosuckers stopped eating ice. Instead, their lights flashed and they began to move towards each other. The Biker Mice hesitated.

'What on earth?' muttered Modo, as slowly but surely all the Snosuckers connected together, linking up to make a giant mechanical man, a Sno-Giant, the size of a small skyscraper. It towered menacingly above the three friends.

'The bigger they are,' said Throttle

'The harder they fall,' Vinnie finished his sentence for him. 'Watch out!'

The Sno-Giant was moving swiftly towards the mice, one enormous foot about to crash down on them.

The frost fighters scattered as the foot came down. CRASH! The Sno-Giant missed the Biker Mice but hit the ice, which cracked loudly. The biker buddies skidded and bounced as the heaving ice played havoc with their cycles. They roared back up to the Sno-Giant, weapons firing; but the giant foot stomped down again, sending up waves of ice and water. The master motorbikers swerved and struggled to keep their balance on the ice floes.

Vinnie blasted up a vertical wall of ice, and took off from the top, his bike roaring. Modo and Throttle kept firing at the Sno-Giant. The machine retaliated swiftly, shooting out a freezing slush-blast that splattered Throttle's wheels. The slush instantly became ice, sending Throttle skidding wildly – Modo raced off after him. Throttle wrestled valiantly with his bike as it shot towards a gaping hole in the ice; he looked doomed, but Modo was thinking fast. He flipped out his arm cannon and, with surgical precision, fired a short, sharp pulse which shattered the ice on his comrade's wheels. Throttle skidded to a halt with an inch to spare.

Limburger was enjoying the scene below him hugely. 'This is the best Christmas show I've ever seen,' he beamed. 'Well done, Karbunkle. Now just finish 'em off, would you dear fellow? We have work to do.'

Karbunkle fiddled desperately with the Sno-Giant control panel. He was sweating despite the cold. 'I am trying, oh Duke of Dairy Produce.' The Sno-Giant meanwhile was smashing up the ice like a demon.

Vinnie had a plan. He fired a grappling hook at the giant android. It sailed through the air and looped around the Sno-Giant's shoulder. Vinnie activated a winch and was suddenly hoisted up in to the air. As Throttle and Modo kept up a steady fire on the Sno-Giant, Vinnie scaled the heights of the robot. He was winched up so fast that when he finally reached the Sno-Giant's shoulder his bike jerked to a halt – and Vinnie went sailing over the handlebars and smacked straight into the side of the automaton's head. Then he slipped.

Far below him his fellow comrades were tiny specks on the ice. 'Bye, Charley. Bye, my snow bro's,' Vinnie cried out as he felt himself losing his grip. He fell. But as he fell, his tail lashed out and wound around a knob on the mechanical man's neck. Vinnie swung back and forth – then, on the next upswing, he dived into the Sno-Giant's ear.

'Roll up for Vinnie's famous trapeze act...' breathed Modo in admiration.

'That's our Vincent,' added Throttle. 'Crazy kid, but loadsa style.'

Vinnie unhitched his tail and looked around him. He was inside the robot's head – a massive command centre filled with dials, winking lights, controls, wires and banks of computers. 'This job calls for intelligence and skill,' said Vinnie to himself. 'Oh, well – too bad!' He ripped a lever out of its socket and began to smash up everything in sight. Sparks flew, smoke billowed, screens shattered and alarms wailed.

The Sno-Giant began tottering about, jerking its arms wildly. Smoke began pouring out of its ears, followed by Vinnie, saboteur extraordinaire. Unhitching his bike from the Giant's shoulder, he jumped onto it and took a flying leap.

Wheee! Vinnie sailed through the air and Whump! landed with a crash on top of the Weatherplane. 'Make room for a little one,' he called cheerfully to the horrified passengers as the plane went spinning off course.

'Help! Save us!' shrieked Karbunkle, Limburger and the Weathermeister – but the Biker Mice were too busy even to laugh. Modo and Throttle were still careering about below as a surge of boiling water from the Sno-Giant melted the ice from beneath Modo's wheels.

'Hey, bro', I'm cookin'!' called Modo. Throttle came to the rescue.

'Better do some fryin' ourselves then,' he announced.

The twosome began to blast the ice out from beneath the Sno-Giant's feet. The Giant staggered, slipped and crashed over into an ungainly somersault. The duo whistled admiringly as the Giant floundered about, sending waves of water and shards of ice flying everywhere. Its eyes flashed and nostrils flared as its metal hands grabbed the air. The Weatherplane spun overhead, still out of control, when CRUNCH! the Sno-Giant grabbed hold of it in its paw. 'Yaaaa!' shrieked the passengers, as the plane started to crumple.

'You – you – you'll be mouse mousse next time we meet!' roared Limburger in a panic-stricken fury.

Vinnie leapt onto his bike and shot off the platform. 'Sorry I can't stay for your just desserts,' he shouted. 'But have a nice winter – and a great fall!'

The Weathermeister struggled to save her equipment while Karbunkle – all his technology forgotten – pounded violently on the Sno-Giant's knuckles. 'Let go you metal moron!' he commanded, but the robot yanked all the more. The villains slid help-lessly up and down the plane as the Weathermeister tore her map and jumbled up all her symbols. The Sno-Giant dangled the plane over a patch of freezing water.

'Karbunkle!' said Limburger breath-lessly. 'I believe a precipitous departure would be prudent at this precise point in time.'

'I beg your pardon, your Camembert Cleverness?'

'GET US OUT OF HERE!'

Karbunkle jumped in shock and his elbow hit the Transporter control. As the Sno-Giant's other hand loomed towards them a crackle of Transporter static flashed between the plane and the Giant – and both vanished from the scene, melting away faster than boiled ice.

The Biker Mice jammed on their brakes and rubbed their eyes.

'Hey! Where'd it go?' protested Modo.

'Just when it was gettin' to be fun,' sighed Vinnie.

'Ya know what?' said Throttle thoughtfully. 'Somethin' tells me Limburger's problems aren't over.'

Limburger Tower shook and bulged as the Weatherplane and the Sno-Giant were transported back to headquarters.

'Couldn't you have left the wretched beast behind?' spluttered Limburger's voice in the darkness.

'I tried,' wailed Karbunkle. 'But...' Karbunkle's explanation was lost in an earth-shattering explosion. The Sno-Giant's arms and legs thrashed out through the walls of the tower. A tremendous blast sent the top three storeys of the building sailing through the air and over the city rooftops. And then . . . silence.

Chapter Seven

A new building, three storeys high, had appeared mysteriously overnight in the orphanage grounds.

'How'd you ever get us this great new home?' a little boy excitedly asked one of three mysterious Santa Clauses.

'Let's just say that it's a kind gift from a very Big Cheese,' winked Santa Throttle, trying to keep his cotton-wool beard in place.

Inside their new home, the orphans dashed about exploring while the other two Santas fixed decorations on a giant tree. Soon all three Santas and the children were gathered around the tree singing carols.

''Twas the night before Christmas,' recited the three Father Christmases together,

'And all through the house

'Not a creature was stirring –

'Apart from the MICE!

'Let's PARTY!'

'It's the Santa Biker Mice!' shrieked the children, recognising their old pals at last.

'Deck the halls with boughs of holly!' sang everyone merrily, their voices floating up to the roof.

And there, high above the excitement, three dark figures clung grimly to a familiar-looking weather vane. The vane had once been part of a weatherplane, but was now embedded in the roof of the new orphanage.

'The outlook is bad und getting vorse,' groaned the Weathermeister, helpless without her maps.

Dr Karbunkle, powerless without his remote control, desperately racked his brains for an escape plan.

Limburger shifted his grip on one of the weather vane's indicators and grimaced as the sweet sound of the carollers floated up to him.

'Ugh! Carol singers – that's all we need! Got any coffee, Karbunkle?'

Jamie Thomson

THE CRYSTAL MAZE CHALLENGE!

Welcome to the fantastic and mysterious world of the Crystal Maze.

Discover the secret of the Maze and take up the challenge, as the Master invites you to test your skills, ingenuity and imagination with fiendish riddles and mind-bending games.

Packed with photographs, facts on the Aztec, Medieval, Industrial and Futuristic Zones, and astonishing crystal amazery, this book is a must for all viewers of the popular TV series, and features a special pull-out games section to play at home.

Andrew Davies

ALFONSO BONZO

Billy Webb was just an ordinary boy. He slept the right way up in bed, and he didn't wear his underpants outside his trousers. But in one way Billy was exceptional – he had a passion for swapping things. He would swap anything, from tropical fish to false moustaches. Privately he thought he might be the best swapper in the world. At least, he did until he met Alfonso Bonzo, the Italian exchange student. Alfonso's idea of swapping went far beyond anything Billy had ever dreamed of.

What followed was funny, strange and sometimes even frightening!

'Very funny . . . powerful as well as entertaining: highly recommended.'
Times Educational Supplement

'Very entertaining and unusual.'
Book Quest

'A very funny book'
The Northern Echo

Ian Strachan

THE UPSIDE DOWN WORLD OF GINGER NUTT

For Ginger the unlikely happens all the time and the impossible becomes the norm.

Ginger is astonished to discover that the cassette recorder he bought in a dingy second-hand shop has a mind of its own. It not only records what people say but can change their words too . . .

Little does Ginger know that it gives him the power not only to cut the school bully down to size but to sort out the crooks who threaten his family.

By the award winning author of *Journey of 1000 Miles*, *The Second Step*, *The Flawed Glass*, *Pebble on the Beach*, *Throwaways* and *Wayne Loves Custard?*

'The fertile imagination of this author produces an unusual, fast-moving feast of fun with clear characterisation and clever ideas. Recommended reading for nine- to twelve-year-olds.'

School Librarian

Colin Dann

THE ANIMALS OF FARTHING WOOD

'We must face the facts!' Toad cried . . . 'Farthing Wood is finished; in another couple of years it won't even exist. We must all find a new home. Now – before it's too late!'

When men arrive with bulldozers in Farthing Wood, its animals and birds know that their world is doomed. The only chance for Badger, Toad, Kestrel and the others is a perilous cross-country trek towards a new life in a nature reserve. But not even Fox, their brave and intelligent leader, is prepared for all the dangers that lie ahead. And when disaster strikes the group, their new home seems an impossible dream. . .

Winner of the Arts Council National Book Award

Nicholas Fisk

THE TALKING CAR

'Boring yourself!' said the voice of the car.
  'What?' said Rob, amazed.

The voice that had only said 'Fasten your seat belts!' was suddenly answering back. Rob and the car become great friends – but what will happen when Rob's father tries to sell the car?

'A lively, fast-moving, warm and comic book . . .'
  Books for Your Children

'This story is original and witty . . . the entire book is a pleasure to read.'

  Lance Salway

A selected list of titles available from Mammoth

While every effort is made to keep prices low. it is sometimes necessary to increase prices at short notice. Mandarin Paperbacks reserves the right to show new retail prices on covers which may differ from those previously advertised in the text or elsewhere.

The prices shown below were correct at the time of going to press.

☐ 7497 0366 0	**Dilly the Dinosaur**	Tony Bradman	£2.50
☐ 7497 0137 4	**Flat Stanley**	Jeff Brown	£2.50
☐ 7497 0306 7	**The Chocolate Touch**	P Skene Catling	£2.50
☐ 7497 0568 X	**Dorrie and the Goblin**	Patricia Coombs	£2.50
☐ 7497 0114 5	**Dear Grumble**	W J Corbett	£2.50
☐ 7497 0054 8	**My Naughty Little Sister**	Dorothy Edwards	£2.50
☐ 7497 0723 2	**The Little Prince (colour ed.)**	A Saint-Exupery	£3.99
☐ 7497 0305 9	**Bill's New Frock**	Anne Fine	£2.99
☐ 7497 0590 6	**Wild Robert**	Diana Wynne Jones	£2.50
☐ 7497 0661 9	**The Six Bullerby Children**	Astrid Lindgren	£2.50
☐ 7497 0319 9	**Dr Monsoon Taggert's Amazing Finishing Academy**	Andrew Matthews	£2.50
☐ 7497 0420 9	**I Don't Want To!**	Bel Mooney	£2.50
☐ 7497 0833 6	**Melanie and the Night Animal**	Gillian Rubinstein	£2.50
☐ 7497 0264 8	**Akimbo and the Elephants**	A McCall Smith	£2.50
☐ 7497 0048 3	**Friends and Brothers**	Dick King-Smith	£2.50
☐ 7497 0795 X	**Owl Who Was Afraid of the Dark**	Jill Tomlinson	£2.99

All these books are available at your bookshop or newsagent, or can be ordered direct from the publisher. Just tick the titles you want and fill in the form below.

Mandarin Paperbacks, Cash Sales Department, PO Box 11, Falmouth, Cornwall TR10 9EN.

Please send cheque or postal order, no currency, for purchase price quoted and allow the following for postage and packing:

UK including BFPO £1.00 for the first book, 50p for the second and 30p for each additional book ordered to a maximum charge of £3.00.

Overseas including Eire £2 for the first book, £1.00 for the second and 50p for each additional book thereafter.

NAME (Block letters) ....

ADDRESS ....

....

☐ I enclose my remittance for ....

☐ I wish to pay by Access/Visa Card Number

Expiry Date